THAT REBELLIC

For
Max Mulvany

That Rebellious Towne

Frances Usher

Illustrated by Gerry Ball

CAMBRIDGE
UNIVERSITY PRESS

Cambridge Reading

General Editors
Richard Brown and Kate Ruttle

Consultant Editor
Jean Glasberg

PUBLISHED BY THE PRESS SYNDICATE OF THE UNIVERSITY OF CAMBRIDGE
The Pitt Building, Trumpington Street, Cambridge CB2 1RP, United Kingdom

CAMBRIDGE UNIVERSITY PRESS
The Edinburgh Building, Cambridge CB2 2RU, United Kingdom
40 West 20th Street, New York, NY 10011-4211, USA
10 Stamford Road, Oakleigh, Melbourne 3166, Australia

First published 1998

Printed in the United Kingdom at the University Press, Cambridge

Typeset in Concorde

A catalogue record for this book is available from the British Library

ISBN 0 521 47705 0 paperback

Contents

Most of the events recounted in this book really happened, although the Berridge family and the Say family are imaginary. I am most grateful to Geoffrey Chapman, author of that excellent account *The Siege of Lyme Regis* (itself based on the diary kept by Edward Drake, who lived through the siege), and to his publishers, Serendip Books, 11 Broad Street, Lyme Regis, for permission to draw on his work.

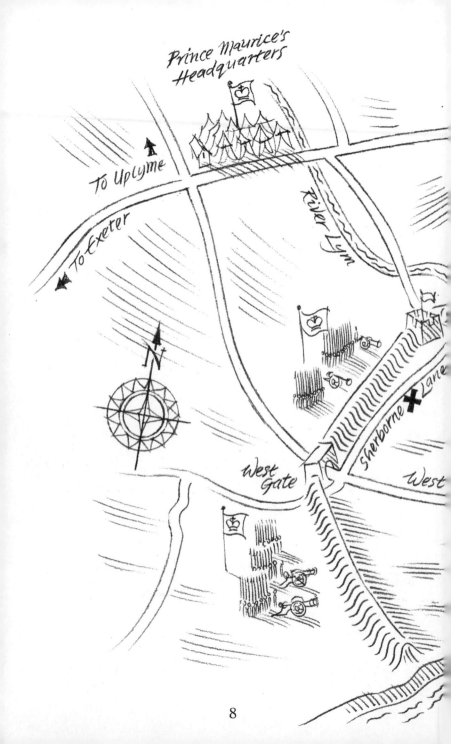

Lyme Regis at the time of the Siege in 1644

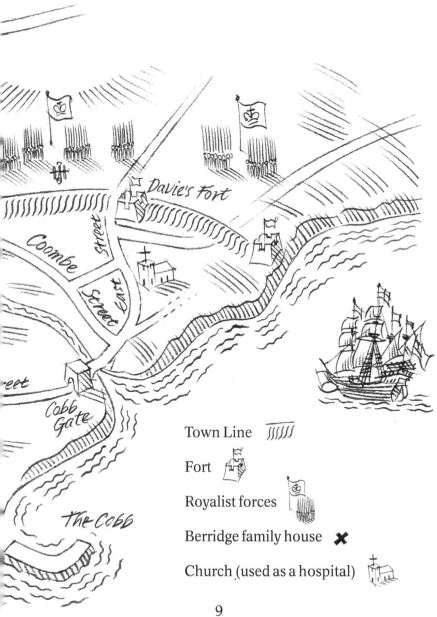

Davie's Fort

Coombe Street

East Street

Cobb Gate

The Cobb

Town Line *JJJJJ*

Fort

Royalist forces

Berridge family house ✖

Church (used as a hospital)

CHAPTER 1

Army on the March

There were soldiers everywhere.

Ann and William and their mother were half-way down the steep field when they heard them. Shouting voices, wheels grinding on a stony track, the clash of hooves.

Thirteen-year-old Ann Say stopped and her arms tightened on the bundle of clothes she was carrying. At the bottom of the field she could see helmets and flags bobbing along behind the trees.

"Mother," she said. "Look down there."

Mistress Say stared down, shading her eyes.

"They're King's men," she said.

They'd all grown good at knowing one army from another. England had been at war for two years now, but it wasn't a war against a foreign army. It was a civil war, a war between people of the same country. It was a struggle between King Charles and his supporters, and Parliament and its supporters. It was about taxes, it was about religion, it was about whether the King could do exactly as he wished or whether Parliament had the right to criticise and control him.

And because this particular civil war was all

about what you thought was right, rather than which part of the country you lived in, or the people you belonged to, almost everyone who became involved in it had to choose which side to be on. And that could be a troublesome matter indeed.

By this April of 1644 it seemed as if the war was to be fought to the death, town against town, friend against friend, father against son. A civil war, where armies roam everywhere, leaves nobody at peace.

Back home on their Somerset farm, the Say family had had soldiers camped on their land for weeks. They'd used the Says' furniture for firewood, they'd stripped the land of every scrap of food. They'd said they'd pay for everything, but they hadn't. They'd simply moved on, leaving the Says with nothing but a damaged, empty shell of a house.

Those had been Parliament soldiers. These today were Royalist – for the King.

"We must pass through them," said Mistress Say. She began to pick her way down the field again.

Ann was standing on one leg.

"This shoe," she said. "Look at it." A piece of leather flapped loose, thick with mud.

Her mother looked back over her shoulder, pushing her hair back under her linen cap.

"You must keep up, Ann," she said. "We needs be into Lyme before nightfall, safe with your uncle and aunt." William was almost at the bottom already,

slipping and sliding down the steep, grassy slope.

"This be Dorset now, I reckon," Ann's mother went on. "Uplyme, maybe. I remember we came here once to pick mushrooms when I was a girl. We must go through the soldiers now, then just up that next big hill and we'll see Lyme."

"Yes, Mother."

The hill on the other side looked even steeper, if that was possible. They'd been walking for nearly a week now, skirting round armies, sleeping in hedges. There'd been so many hills.

"Will the soldiers stop us, Mother?"

Mistress Say smiled a thin smile. "Who knows? The Lord will go before us. Like a strong light, Ann."

"Yes, Mother."

Ann hitched her skirts out of the mud and went on down the field, towards the sound of hooves.

"Through here, William. Quickly, quickly." Mistress Say darted through a gap in the column of foot-soldiers, pulling Ann with her. But William lingered by the hedge, staring.

Thousands of them, he thought. There are thousands.

They were marching three and four abreast along the sunken track. Dusty, mud-coloured men, some bearing muskets, some pikes. A troop of Horse was up in front and another was behind, riding out of the little wood. The column seemed to go on and on and on. Where were they all going?

He watched the straining muscles of two horses dragging a heavy gun. "Demi-culverin," he said out loud.

His brother Rufus had taught him the names of guns. Rufus, who had run away to join Lord Powlett's army. Where was Rufus now? Fighting for the King somewhere. They'd had no news of him for months.

"Demi-culverin nothing," a voice growled.

A gunner was glaring at William. The column had stopped. Further up the line a cart-wheel was stuck in the mud.

"That's a full culverin, you young weasel." The man's face was streaked with black grease. "How old be you?"

"Twelve," said William.

"Old enough to know, then. A full culverin, I tell 'ee."

"Aye, I see now," said William. "A range of –

what? A thousand yards?"

"Two thousand, more like. Send a twenty-pound ball through anything, that would. Like this." The man's fist smashed down. "We're with Prince Maurice here. Prince Maurice will show 'em."

"Show who?"

"The King's enemies. That pock-marked, scurvy hotbed of rebels down there. They been asking for trouble." His head jerked towards the huge hill. "T'other side o' that. Down there in Lyme."

"Lyme?" said William. "We're going to Lyme."

The gunner stared at him.

"My mother was born there," said William. "We've got no home now, so we go to her brother, Master Thomas Berridge of Lyme."

The man laughed, savagely. "You won't be down there long, weasel."

The column was moving off. "Why?" called William, running after the gunner. "Why won't we be?"

"Because we'll blow you out of it," the man shouted back, lashing at the horses. "Nobody won't be left alive in Lyme come next week."

The sounds of the army had faded in the spring afternoon. Ann could hear a lark singing overhead.

The three of them struggled up to the brow of the great hill.

"There," said Mistress Say, dropping her bundle

15

on the grass. "There's Lyme."

Still panting, Ann looked.

At the foot of the hill the little town spilled towards the sea. Ann saw a huddle of thatched roofs and wisps of chimney smoke and a square grey church tower. Beyond that, soft golden cliffs curved around the sea.

She drew a deep breath, gazing out across the whole sweep of sparkling, dancing blue water.

Surely nothing bad could happen to them in such a lovely place.

CHAPTER 2

Earthworks and Trumpets

It was the next day. In the house in Sherborne Lane in Lyme, the Berridge household had gathered for midday dinner.

"Bless this our meat and drink, Lord . . . ," said Uncle Thomas Berridge, sitting at the head of the table.

Ann stood by the fire with a pile of plates in her hands, looking round at these relatives she'd never met before. Her cousin Judah's eyes were closed, her head bent, but her hand still quietly stirred the big pot of stew that hung over the flames. Her hair was neat and smooth, her grey gown and white cap spotlessly clean.

At the table William sat between his mother and eleven-year-old Deb. Ann saw Deb turn and dart him a small smile, her dark curls bouncing. Aunt Mercy Berridge, small, stout, grey-haired, gave Ann a cold stare. Ann hastily closed her eyes.

"Protect this town now, O Lord," prayed Uncle Thomas. "Strike down Charles Stuart, that man of pride."

That was how he often referred to King Charles.

Uncle Thomas might be quite a gentle, kind man, thought Ann, but the Berridges were still a Puritan family, stern, plain-living, strict about their religion. And they disapproved of the King as they disapproved of many things, even of dancing and singing. Unless it was singing hymns, of course. Uncle Thomas had no time for kings, or earls, or bishops. He believed that nobody, not even the King, had a right to call himself by a title, or raise himself above others.

"Let not this man seek to rule our land with his power alone," his uncle was saying. "Raise up Parliament to protect the people. Guard us all against Charles Stuart and his hosts of the ungodly. Amen."

"Amen," said Aunt Berridge. "Pass the plates." She dipped her ladle into the pot of stew.

"Aye, hosts of the ungodly," her husband repeated to himself. "But we will stand firm now the day of battle is at hand."

Ann, going round the table with plates of stew, shivered. A battle couldn't come today. Not on their first day in Lyme.

"Judah." Aunt Berridge looked at her older daughter. "We must take bandages to the church, and then make more. There will be many wounds before long."

"Aye, Mother." Judah smiled at Ann. "And you too, Ann," she said.

"William must come with us to the Town Line," said Uncle Thomas. "We need every able-bodied man today."

The Town Line. Ann knew what her uncle meant. She'd seen the Town Line last evening when they'd come into Lyme.

It had been almost dark by then, because they'd all become so weary and footsore. But they'd stopped and stared when they'd seen what was happening.

Dozens of men, and women too, were toiling by lantern-light to dig a trench right across the street. The earth was being thrown up into a great wall.

"Earthworks," Mistress Say had said. "There's to be fighting, then."

"Against that army we saw today?" asked William.

19

"Aye."

"Against the King," said a woman, overhearing. She was resting, gasping a little, on her heavy shovel. She looked up at them with bright eyes. "Lyme is standing solid for Parliament," she said. "Now, pass through and let us go on with the work."

As they stepped through a gap, Ann saw the wall stretched each way into the distance. Lyme was being sealed off against the invaders.

"Mother –"

"Make haste."

And Mistress Say had led Ann and William to her brother's house in Sherborne Lane, and the three of them had somehow been squeezed in for the night.

But Ann, in the big bed next to Judah and Deb, had lain awake for hours. Carts rattled past the window, footsteps hurried by. Lyme was labouring to finish the Town Line before the enemy struck.

"Come, Judah, to the church."

Aunt Berridge pushed away her plate and stood up. Ann's mother quickly did the same.

"And Deb and Ann. There will be mattresses to fill ... bandages to prepare ... "

Deb made a face. "I would like to help dig the earthworks," she said.

"What?"

Aunt Berridge's eyes popped and her grey hair quivered indignantly. She shook Deb.

"Only rough women do that," she said. "To the

church, miss, this minute, to make ready for the wounded. Come, Ann."

Slowly, Ann followed her out. Why did no-one ask her if she wanted to help with this battle?

Behind her, the door slammed and William hurried down the garden path, pulling on his coat. Ann stood still at the gate, listening to the birds singing in the trees, the little River Lym gurgling in the sunshine.

"Move, Ann," said William. "I must go to the Line."

Ann glanced up at the steep cliffs behind the town. Somewhere up there an army was waiting. Waiting to start killing.

She shook her head. "I thought we came here for peace," she said. "Not fighting."

William wasn't listening. "I must go to the Line quickly," he said. "Uncle has been explaining it to me. The sea protects one side of the town. This great earth wall with forts spaced along it, forts full of soldiers, will protect the rest. But Uncle says the enemy have more soldiers than us, and great culverins like I saw yesterday. The enemy –"

"They're not our enemy," said Ann. "What about Rufus?"

"Rufus?" William said blankly.

"Our brother Rufus. Have you forgotten he's fighting for the King? Are you going to help the King's enemies? But you and I need not be on either side, William. Let others have enemies if they want to. King . . . Parliament . . . Why must they fight?"

"Ann!" called her mother from the lane.

"You're but a girl," said William. "It is natural you would be afraid. Go with Mother and prepare for the wounded. We will protect you when the enemy come."

They came that evening.

William had been on the Line all afternoon, shovelling earth. When the enemy came, he was leaning on his shovel, sucking his blistered thumb.

"You gurt softie," said a man hacking out soil at the bottom of the trench. "Mighty use you'll be when Prince Maurice strikes."

William flushed. Back home on the farm in Somerset he'd been used to digging. He'd had to get used to it when first his father had died of fever, and then Rufus had left home. But a trench and a wall that was nearly a mile round – that was different.

"Want to try it down here, lad? Come on."

William shook his head. His task was easier. All he had to do was pick up the earth that came flying up from the bottom and throw it high on to the walls they were building. But his hands were already split and blistered. And the walls were so tall, as tall as he was.

"These walls are but a molehill." A man in a blue

coat spat into the dust. "A child could still jump
over. We should make them higher and not so long."

"But they must be long to protect the whole
town," argued Uncle Thomas Berridge. "We cannot
leave houses outside at the enemy's mercy."

"But how shall we defend such a long wall?"

"With the Lord's help," said Thomas Berridge.
"Let other towns declare for the enemy if they wish.

Lyme has always stood firm for Parliament, even if we stand alone. The Lord will not desert us now – " He broke off. "What is that shouting?"

It was coming from the top of the street. William looked up. He was just in time to see two or three young men racing down, yelling as they came.

"Man the Line! They are upon us. Man the Line!"

Uncle Thomas stepped forward and grasped the largest young man by the arm.

"Solomon? What news?"

"They're coming, Father," Solomon Berridge panted. "Do you not see? Or hear? Look up there."

Even as he spoke a blare of trumpets sounded from the cliffs above the town. William gazed up.

The cliffs had come to life. Outlined against the sky, an army was being paraded. Banners . . . horses . . . cannons. And soldiers. Shouting, jeering soldiers.

"You down there in Lyme . . ."

"Surrender . . . Surrender . . ."

"Stinking rebels . . ."

"Traitors! We'll bury you . . . before breakfast . . ."

"Surrender!"

"Surrender!"

The sky was black with them. William said, "There are thousands of them."

"Indeed," said his uncle. "Certainly four thousand, perhaps six. It is hard to tell."

"And Lyme?"

"We have soldiers stationed here and some fine commanders. Why, Captain Thomas Pyne – "

"How many soldiers?"

"Only fifteen hundred," admitted his uncle. "But the people of Lyme will fight alongside them, every man and boy."

William looked at the earthworks, and suddenly they seemed to him useless against such numbers, such massive guns. They would blow them all to pieces, as the gunner had said. His heart froze with fear.

An elbow dug his ribs.

"Lost your voice, Cousin Will?"

Laughing, Solomon tipped back his head and made a funnel with his hands.

"Hey! You up there! Come down and fight!"

"Fight!"

"They don't dare come down . . ."

"Fight!"

Suddenly, all round William, people were shouting and gesturing at the enemy. He saw an old man almost dancing in the street. He saw Aunt Berridge, scarlet-faced, shaking her fist at the cliff.

"Fight!"

"Fight!"

"Fight!"

Now William was shouting with the rest. So Lyme was smaller than the enemy. What did that matter? Lyme folk could beat anyone. It would be like the Bible story, David beating the giant Goliath.

"William – "

Ann was struggling through the crowd, her cloak pulled round her. She looked pale.

"Have no fear, Ann," called William. "We'll fight for you, Solomon and me and the rest."

His cousin Solomon was twenty-one. He and his friends had sailed right across the ocean to Newfoundland many times, fishing. What was a King's army to them?

"Ann, have no fear," he said again.

She looked at him.

"I think you have lost your wits," she said. "All of you." She turned away and vanished in the crowd.

All that night enemy camp-fires blazed along the cliffs.

To the townsfolk, slaving below to finish the earthworks, they looked no more than the dancing lights of tiny fireflies.

CHAPTER 3

Rat in a Trap

The capture of Lyme should have been a very minor matter. That's what the Royalists thought.

After all, a King's officer could stand on the cliffs above the town and look down with his perspective glass, and see the gulls on the roofs and the dogs in the streets. Lyme – what was it? A shabby little place of no importance at all.

True, there was a low earth wall round the town, but what was that? A short barrage of gunfire, and Lyme would be howling for mercy. That would teach it to pit itself against His Most Sacred Majesty King Charles, against this splendid army commanded by the King's own nephew, Prince Maurice.

Yes, thought the Royalists. The battle of Lyme would surely be over by suppertime.

Down on the Town Line, things seemed different. Everything was ready now. Everyone was waiting.

William stood in his place beside Solomon. He was holding his cousin's two-foot-long smouldering match for him, ready for when Solomon wanted to fire.

"When will they come, Sol?" He climbed up on the rough step and craned his head over the earthworks.

"Keep down." Solomon grabbed his cousin's jerkin. "Do you want those Frenchies to blow your head off?"

"Are there Frenchmen up there?" William gazed up at Solomon, tall, broad-shouldered, hands relaxed on his musket, face weather-beaten from the sea. There could scarcely be a bigger, stronger man the whole length of the Line, he thought proudly.

"Frenchmen, Cornish, Irish." Solomon shrugged. "All sorts of foreigners. Some dragged there against

their will, of course. But there are real soldiers too, I heard. Like Lord Powlett's lot."

William opened his mouth, closed it again.

"Rufus is with Lord Powlett," he said at last.

Solomon cocked an eyebrow at him. "Aye?"

William nodded.

He was remembering. First, Father had died so suddenly. Rufus had tried to run the farm, to take Father's place. But he and Mother had argued about everything. William could still hear their angry voices, coming from downstairs late into the night sometimes.

Then one day they heard Lord Powlett was raising an army from their district, to fight for the King. And Rufus, whose whole heart had seemed until then to be in the land, in their flocks of sheep and their fine orchard of cider-apple trees, had just gone off one night without saying anything to anyone and joined it. His older brother Rufus, until then the most peaceable person William had known.

At the beginning they'd had a couple of short, mud-stained letters from him. Then nothing. Mother never talked about Rufus now.

"Well, 'tis a monstrous big army up there," Solomon was saying. "We'll not see Rufus, I'll warrant."

They fell into silence. Solomon rubbed up his matchlock musket stock. William sorted out bullets. Over to the west they could hear snatches of gunfire and see a heavy cloud of smoke. Defenders were already skirmishing with the enemy there.

William glanced along their silent trench, at the line of grim-faced men, waiting.

"When the enemy do come," he said, "we'll be ready for them. Won't we, Sol?"

The firing went on all night as the enemy closed in, keeping Ann awake.

By morning she was weary and sore-eyed. She sat in the empty church with Judah and Deb, filling mattresses with straw, ready for the wounded when they arrived.

"Just three more." Judah nipped off her thread neatly. Judah did everything neatly, Ann thought, watching her start to stitch up the next filled mattress. "Then we can have twenty mattresses along this side, sixteen along here . . ."

"And I shall nurse the wounded," said Deb. "When the surgeon needs to bleed them, I shall hold the bowl. You too, Ann."

Ann didn't answer. She shook her mattress down and thrust in another handful of straw.

"The surgeon will not want such a flibbertigibbet to help him," Judah reproved her young sister. At seventeen, Judah was very grown up. "When the wounded are brought in . . ."

Ann got up and went to lean against the open door. The grass outside in the churchyard was very green.

Must they talk all the time of the wounded? she thought. I wish I was at home.

The guns were still firing. Her head throbbed. Then there was a new sound. Voices, coming rapidly closer.

"That's Mother," said Judah.

She got to her feet and came to stand at the door with Ann. Aunt Mercy Berridge was hurrying up the church path, talking over her shoulder to two men. The men carried a stretcher between them.

"Wounded!" said Deb, eyes shining, as they came inside.

She put out an eager hand to the figure on the stretcher. Then she drew it back hastily.

There was a thick wet red stain where the man's face should have been. Ann felt her stomach churn.

Judah asked quietly, "Shall I run for the surgeon, Mother?"

"No." Aunt Mercy took her fingers from the man's wrist. "We are too late."

She pulled the blanket over.

"Go to your work now."

"What – what happened?" asked Ann.

"He was a man defending the Line," said her aunt. "He stood up to see the enemy better. They were firing and – " She spread her hands. "He was doing the Lord's work. He is in Paradise now."

She nodded to the men to pick up the stretcher.

"You will see worse soon, child," she said. "Very soon."

In the next few days the enemy came closer, capturing land, setting up their huge guns, tightening their hold on the town.

On dark nights Solomon and his friends went out raiding enemy camps. William would hear them coming back at dawn, feet stamping, chanting in triumph:

"Lyme! . . . Lyme! . . . Lyme! . . . LYME! . . ."

Looking out, William would see them down in the lane. Half a dozen young men, white teeth

32

laughing in their blackened faces, clothes torn.

"Look what we've captured this time, Father! How's that for spoils of war?"

They brought back sixteen muskets one morning. Another time it was pickaxes with the King's initials, C R, carved on the handles. Once, it was a huge shoulder of mutton.

"That'll feed half Lyme," exulted Solomon. "Captain Thomas Pyne congratulated us specially."

"Solomon, you didn't – " For once, William's mother spoke up. "You didn't kill anyone up there, did you?"

William shot her a glance. She must have heard that Lord Powlett's army was up there.

Solomon shrugged. "One or two, Aunt Joan. It is necessary to get past their sentries sometimes. Maybe three."

"Oh, more. Six . . ."

"Seven . . ."

"Eight . . ."

They were laughing, slapping each other's backs. William stared at his cousin's big hands, strong from pulling on oars and ropes at sea. Now those hands had squeezed a trigger – or perhaps a man's throat – in the dark. What would that feel like?

Still the enemy closed in.

They launched attacks on the forts where the Lyme soldiers were stationed, setting up batteries of their own from which to fire. By 25th April they were within a pistol shot of the West Gate. The townsfolk responded by heaping up earth and stones three or four yards thick against the inside of the gate. Next day Captain Marsh, commander of the West fort, was killed by a shot that flew in through a look-out hole in the fort's walls. On the 27th, the enemy were seen to be working on another huge battery, this time on the east side of the town, ready to menace Davie's Fort. Alarmed, Captain Davie ordered his men to thicken the wall on that side to eight feet. And still the enemy advanced.

On Sunday 28th April, a hush fell. The Royalists' loop about the town was complete. Lyme was under siege, its people caught like a rat in a trap.

The King's army waited for Prince Maurice to give the signal to attack.

And at last it came.

CHAPTER 4

Not Like Them

Trumpets sounded, drums rattled. In the Royalists' tight-packed ranks the King's foot-soldiers exchanged uneasy glances and gripped their pikes more firmly. Horses tossed their heads, harnesses jingled. The officers sat bolt upright in their saddles, staring ahead. Everyone was awaiting the signal.

A moment of silence. Then . . .

"CHAAAARGE!"

A harsh yell burst from hundreds of throats. The front row moved off, stumbling a little under the weight of helmet and breastplate, jostled by those behind.

"Forward there! Go forward, man," roared an officer of Horse, leaning from his saddle and raising his whip against a young foot-soldier. But the soldier had seen what lay ahead and his courage had gone.

They were being marched towards a line of earthworks – and a line of muskets. Straight towards the guns.

"Come on there," yelled the officers. "Come *on*, dunderheads, shout! FOR THE KING! THE KING!"

But other, different, voices were coming from the earth walls:

"The Lord our strength!"

"Salvation! Salvation!"

"Lyme! . . . Lyme! . . . Lyme! . . . LYME!"

In the Royalist ranks a man fell, moaning. Then another and another. Their comrades wavered, stood still.

"Forward, damn you! FORWARD!"

William never forgot it.

He stood on the Line and he went on doing the right things: handing Solomon lengths of lighted match, passing over more bullets. But through the smoke he caught glimpses of the enemy, and what he saw shocked him.

Their officers were driving on the men like cattle to the slaughter, cursing, slashing at them with their whips. He saw one man fend off the blows with his arm, and then duck and run back up the street and away out of sight.

"They're a rabble of whey-faced cowards," he cried to Solomon over the firing. "All of them."

"Not all," Solomon shouted back. "Some of them'll give their lives for the King. You'll see one day."

William folded his mouth stubbornly.

"A filthy rabble. They're not like us. Here in Lyme we all stand together. Not like them."

Night fell. The enemy withdrew. Lyme had survived.

The first stars appeared over the Cobb, that thick curved wall that protected Lyme from the sea. Two ships slipped quietly in and anchored. They were laden with a hundred extra soldiers and food for the besieged town.

In the makeshift hospital the wounded lay on the floor, waiting their turn. A man with shattered legs rolled his head from side to side, groaning and sobbing. Another, his face caked with blood, stared sightlessly up at Judah as she held his hand.

Ann was trying to spoon warm broth into a man's mouth, but his lips twisted and the broth trickled down his chin. Behind her a preacher was praying over a captured Royalist soldier, urging him to think of his sins before he died. In the corner, Ann's mother was helping to hold a man down as the surgeon probed his arm for a bullet. The man screamed like a rabbit and a sickly, dreadful smell began to fill the room.

"Ann." Aunt Berridge touched her arm. "They need help to unload the ships. To the Cobb now, you and Deb."

She hustled them to the door. Deb drew a deep breath.

"Ah, good air at last. Come, Ann." She looked back. "What ails you, Ann?"

"I will not unload ships," said Ann.

Deb stared at her. "But it's a good task, a wholesome task after . . . ," she gestured back, ". . . after that." Her face wrinkled in disgust.

"I know," said Ann. She shook her head. She couldn't explain.

She just knew she would nurse the wounded because you couldn't leave the wounded to die. And perhaps, too, because it was awful and unwholesome, as Deb said. It made her feel a little better to do something so difficult.

But unloading ships was different. That would be helping the war to go on. And why should she do that? If everyone refused, the fighting would stop. Then they could all go back to doing sensible things like working in the fields and fishing in the sea. And once the fighting stopped, she and her family could go home and rebuild their lives. War was cruel and wrong and silly.

"I think you are wicked," said Deb. "There are babies here who will starve without food. Old people. Do you want to kill them?"

"No," said Ann. "It's just – "

"If they die, it will be your fault," Deb said.

Ann gave in. But as she and Deb struggled that night along the stony beach, dragging between them a large sack full of bread and yellow cheeses, she was telling herself fiercely, "No more. Just nursing the wounded and unloading food. That's all."

The weather changed. Driving rain set in. Outside the walls the enemy went quiet, sheltering from the wet under canvas and sacks.

Days passed.

A prayer had started to form inside Ann's head. It was there all the time: as she sliced bread with Aunt Berridge, as she helped Judah wash someone's festering wound, as she dropped wearily into bed each night.

"Let it be finished. Let them give up now, Lord, and just go away."

But would her prayer be answered?

CHAPTER 5

Fog

On Monday 6th May, thick fog came rolling in from the sea.

"Ugh." Solomon pulled his tall black hat down over his face. "I hate fog. Hated it at sea, hate it now. Those demons will come creeping up on us. You'll see."

They stood all day at their posts, shivering in the clammy air, straining their eyes towards the silent enemy positions. Nothing happened.

By evening most of them had laid down their muskets and were lounging in the trench smoking their pipes.

"Supper," someone said. "They'll not come now."

They left one or two men on sentry duty, and the rest of them piled into the taverns of Lyme.

William was sitting on a stool by an ale-house fire, a tankard of ale before him, just biting into a large turnip pie, when the shout came.

"Back to the Line!"

"The devils have broke through!"

"They're in the town!"

"To the Line . . . the Line!"

William dropped the pie and joined in the rush. Men were running from every doorway and alley. He skidded round the corner of Coombe Street, pounded up the hill . . . and stopped dead.

Solomon was in the middle of the street, fighting hand to hand with two Royalists. William saw him swing his musket like a club, saw one of the men fumble for the dagger at his belt.

"Sol –"

His cousin twisted his head. "Get on the Line," he shouted. "Stop 'em breaking through. Go on, Will, the Line."

William hesitated. Then he ran.

It was nearly dark now and the fog was thicker than ever. He stumbled along the street, slipping and sliding on the cobbles. He could hear gunfire ahead, and screams coming from the Line.

It was a desperate situation. Too late now to say that they should have stayed on watch. The enemy were through in three places and were fighting their way, minute by minute, towards the centre of the town.

"Fall on," they cried. "Fall on, the day is ours!"

"The town is ours!"

"For the King!"

" . . . the King . . ."

Ann was on her way home from the hospital when it happened. She and her mother and aunt had just turned the corner into West Street.

"More powder!" a man shouted to them as he ran past.

"For the love of God, woman, more charge. We run short."

Ann gripped her mother's arm. Wild-eyed men were struggling to hold the Line, grappling hand to hand with enemy soldiers intent on crossing it.

The air was thick with fog and smoke. Someone tossed a grenade and an enemy soldier toppled down, screaming. Ann saw William among the defenders, waving a pike and shouting.

"More powder from the store!"

"Run, mistress, run."

Aunt Berridge was pushing her.

"Did you not hear, child? Run to the powder store and we'll follow."

"Quickly, quickly," her mother urged. "They will overrun the town."

"Let them," said Ann. She turned to face the two women. "Then the fighting will stop."

Her mother covered her mouth. "How can you speak so? After your uncle has taken us in, your kind aunt . . ."

"Ungrateful chit." Her aunt grasped her arm. Her mouth was tight, her chin shaking with anger. "Do you not understand? We are at war, girl, war. Whose side are you on? Ours or theirs?"

"I am on no side," Ann began. "All I want – "

Then she stopped, staring over her aunt's shoulder.

That young soldier, gripping the Royalist standard, the leader of the group struggling to cross. Wasn't it Rufus?

But, even as she strained to see, the billowing smoke hid him again.

It couldn't have been.

Could it?

Her aunt was shaking her.

"I say again, miss. Whose side are you on?"

"No side," said Ann. "None."

She turned and walked away.

The Royalist attack on the Line had been a brave one. But it failed.

Men lay where they dropped until at last the attackers were beaten back. Then the defenders went out and began to count.

One Lyme man dead. Only one. Perhaps a hundred Royalists, including Colonel Francis Blewett, one of the King's best commanders.

"A proud day for Lyme," gloated Solomon. "And see, Father, these wounds in his back. I'll warrant his own side did this. They hate their officers so."

"Then Lyme will show them how to behave," his father said quietly.

Next day the two sides met for a parley. Colonel Blewett's body, decently washed and in a coffin, was handed over to his own side for burial. The Royalists asked if they should pay.

"Take it," said the men of Lyme. "We are not so poor that we cannot give it to you."

Then the parley ended, the two sides separated and the siege went on.

CHAPTER 6

Tired to Death

Time passed.

I've been here for ever, Ann sometimes thought. In this town, shut inside these walls.

East Street . . . West Street . . . Sherborne Lane . . . Coombe Street. Little streets and alleys, dusty and hot, choked day and night with smoke. That was Lyme under siege. You could go round and round inside the walls like a squirrel in a cage. But you couldn't go out, to find a place where the sky was blue and the sea sparkled.

At home I'd be out in the orchard now, thought Ann. The birds would be singing. I'd see grass and flowers everywhere.

At home.

Sometimes William thought of home, too. Like on the day of the thunderstorm.

He and Solomon crouched in their trench under a piece of canvas as the lightning flashed and the rain teemed down. "We'll not see much more fighting today," said Solomon, easing himself into a more comfortable position. "Not in this plaguey weather."

William wasn't sorry. He'd been on the Line day after day for weeks, and was growing weary.

"We could play a hand of cards," he said. But Lyme preachers disapproved of cards, calling them the Devil's picture-book.

The rain settled into drizzle and William got up to stretch his legs. The enemy seemed quiet. What were they doing?

He glanced back at Sol and saw he was dozing, hat over his eyes. Then he pulled himself up the earth walls and looked over.

It was disappointingly ordinary. Just soaking wet fields criss-crossed by trenches, trenches just like Lyme's. There were tents in the distance and horses grazing.

He jerked his head back. Something – someone – had moved in the nearest trench. So there were soldiers in there waiting for the rain to stop, just as on William's side they were waiting.

A man stood up, pushing back his wet hair with an impatient hand, staring across towards the sea.

Rufus. Was it? It was really not close enough to tell. But Rufus did push his hair back like that. On hot days when he was haymaking, or in winter, out riding round the farm. Just like that.

At home.

Then the enemy's tactics changed. Attacking the walls and the forts had won them nothing but a bloody nose. What now?

"The Cobb," decided Uncle Thomas. "They'll go for the ships soon." The supply ships sent by Parliament with extra men or rations were Lyme's lifeline.

Sure enough, the day came when they noticed heavy guns, culverins and demi-culverins, being moved on the cliffs to face the Cobb.

"They'll never hit the ships," said Solomon. "They lie too far off shore."

Perhaps. But they could destroy the small boats that went back and forth unloading them.

An extra guard was put on the Cobb, day and night. Among those chosen for night duty was William.

"But the boy needs to sleep," protested his mother. "He is on the Line all day."

"We can all sleep," said his aunt grimly, "when this siege is lifted."

So each evening when William came off the Line, he'd eat a hasty supper and go down to the Cobb.

At first he rather enjoyed it. The nights were warm, the sea air fresh. He and the other lads would perch on a boat, their Lyme banners flapping overhead, and tell stories to keep themselves awake. Who needed sleep?

But on the fourth night, suddenly William's eyes grew heavy and he couldn't stop yawning. A lad called Barty was already asleep in one of the barges.

William found himself a corner too.

When he woke the sun was up. And the Lyme banners had gone, stolen by the enemy while the boys slept.

William was full of shame. The enemy would be displaying the banners by now in one of their camps.

"'Tis only keeping awake, young beggar," growled the old men of the town. "If you don't watch out, they might set fire to the boats next time."

But next time was worse even than that.

William had just gone off night duty. There'd been no sound from the guns yet and it was a calm, sunny morning. He paused to watch a small boat being rowed in towards Cobb Gate. It was weighed down with 300 bushels of pease and malt. Gulls wheeled round, calling. It was very peaceful.

The explosion came without warning. Spray flew up. There were shouts, and one dreadful scream.

The man at the oars fell forward, his head split open, the brains sliding out. Nobody had time to reach him. The boat sank within a minute.

William and Barty joked about it afterwards. Barty even mimicked the way the man fell, clutching at the air, and William laughed. But inside he didn't feel like laughing. Inside, he felt sick.

Somehow, he went on feeling sick, though he didn't tell anyone. He went on the Line that morning as usual. The guns around the Cobb boomed all day. Inside William's head the oarsman screamed and the boat sank, again and again and again.

At seven that evening he was called back to the Cobb. There'd been another attack. The Royalists, both Horse and Foot, were pouring down the hill towards the Cobb, hurling flaming torches at the boats.

"Wildfire!"

"Beware wildfire!"

Outnumbered, the Lyme men were forced back. Under Captain Thomas Pyne's command they tried a desperate counter-charge. But, by the end of that night, nearly all their boats had been destroyed, and six Lyme men lay dead or dying. Among them was Captain Thomas Pyne himself.

He was carried to the hospital, still breathing, but grey-faced.

It was Lyme's darkest hour so far.

"A most valiant man, Captain Pyne," said Uncle Thomas.

"Aye." A sigh went round the room.

From the corner where he sat forgotten, William looked round.

Eight men, Lyme's leading citizens, were squeezed into the Berridges' tiny parlour. They were holding a council of war.

"The Captain cannot recover," said the Governor. "We have lost one of our finest leaders."

"And we are losing men. If this continues . . ."

"We shall fight on until the end," said the Governor.

"Of course."

"And then cut our way out."

Silence.

"If only the enemy did not know how few we are," said someone.

"They see gaps in the Line and it makes them bolder, striking everywhere. The walls, the forts, the Cobb . . ."

"We cannot hide from them how few we are."

"And how tired."

"Tired to death."

The door opened. Aunt Berridge came in with a jug of ale. Behind her came Judah with a trayful of tankards, and Deb and Ann with bread and cheese.

"Plain fare, gentlemen," Aunt apologised. "Food runs short."

"Indeed," said the Governor, pouring ale. "My pardon for taking your rations. But we needs keep up our strength. The Line must be defended to the last man."

"Or woman," said Uncle Thomas.

Another silence, a different one this time.

"What can you mean, husband?" said Aunt Berridge at last.

"I mean," said Uncle Thomas, "that women must come on the Line to fight alongside the men."

"Fight? With a musket?" Aunt Berridge drew the three girls to her. "That is against nature. A woman should work at home or in the hospital."

"The men are dying," said Uncle Thomas. "And

we are exhausted. We need the women. Do we not, Judah?"

"Aye, Father." Judah was pale but her voice was firm. "I shall be on the Line tomorrow."

"Good maid." Uncle Thomas smiled at his daughter. "And Deb – "

Deb gave a skip of delight.

"No . . ." said Aunt Berridge.

"Yes." Uncle Thomas sighed and stood up. "Even the youngest cannot be spared. We shall expect all three of them tomorrow, Judah and Deb and Ann."

William looked across at Ann. He saw her hands were clenched and she was breathing fast.

She isn't going to do it, he thought. Ann's going to say no. And quite right too. Who wants women on the Line?

But the moment passed. Uncle Thomas was already leading the others out.

"All three of them," he said again. "On the Line, ready to fight, at day-break."

The door closed. William and Ann were left staring at each other.

CHAPTER 7

Well Defended

It was a warm, hazy Sunday afternoon. Eight large ships lay at anchor in the bay.

They were commanded by the Lord High Admiral of the Parliamentary navy, and had been there for three days now. The town's desperate plight had been eased.

If Ann and her mother had had time, they might have admired the pennants fluttering from the masts, or stopped to listen to the creak of timbers as the tide turned once more. But the two of them were hurrying to the Line and it was too smoky to see much.

Anyway, they were walking in a trench. The enemy had started firing on the town itself now, smashing chimneys, blowing roofs off, killing people in the streets. So a network of trenches had been hastily dug to walk in, dark and smelly, trampled with mud from the hundreds of feet that went up and down day and night.

"Have a care for those new shoes, Ann," warned Mistress Say.

Ann glanced down. The red shoes weren't really new. When the Admiral's sailors had seen how ill-clothed and hungry everyone in the town was, they'd made a collection round the ships. They'd handed over their sailors' rations and a huge heap of boots and shoes. Ann had thrown away her old broken shoes and taken a pair. They almost fitted her if she walked carefully.

"Now –"

They were at the Line. Mistress Say stood waiting. And Ann, looking at her, suddenly seeing her, burst out laughing.

"I'm sorry, Mother," she spluttered. "But you look so . . . so . . ."

Mistress Say flushed, smoothing down her skirts nervously, straightening the tall black hat perched uncertainly on her head.

"I cannot help it, Ann," she said. "Your uncle has requested it."

"I know," said Ann. "It's just – "

It was a trick they were playing on the enemy. It would never do, Uncle Thomas explained, for Prince Maurice to guess that Lyme had run short of men and had had to call women to the Line. So the women were ordered to wear men's hats when they were within enemy sight.

Some of them – rough, godless women, her aunt said – wore men's breeches and boots as well. But that was too much for Ann's mother. It was all she could do to wear the man's headgear.

"We make a good pair," said Ann. "Me slopping along in these scarlet shoes, you hatted like a – a journeyman tooth-puller." She pulled the corners of her mouth down dolefully, and clapped her own hat on her head.

"Come, Mother," she said. "Into battle."

Reluctantly, her mother smiled.

"Oh, Ann," she said. "And on the Sabbath too. What war makes us do."

Indeed, thought Ann.

Who would have dreamt that Ann Say would wear a man's hat and fight on the front line against a King's army? Yet she'd done it for three days now and was starting to feel she'd done it for years.

"Good day, Mistress Ann."

The musketeer she'd been told to help, Master John Sampson, smiled and gave her a hand out of the trench. He was a quiet, middle-aged man, a tailor in normal life.

There was a lull in the fighting for the moment. Ann started to hand little powder tubes to Master Sampson to tuck into his bandolier, the leather strap worn across his shoulder. Behind him she glimpsed her mother, gingerly picking up a length of smouldering match. Ann smiled to herself.

Smiling? On the Line, where at any minute she might be ordered to kill somebody? She couldn't believe how light-hearted she felt.

Master Sampson took a quick look across the earthworks.

"Time to show yourself," he said to Ann.

She climbed up on to the step for a moment, so that her black hat showed.

"Enough. Down again," said Master Sampson. "They will be counting the hats and think us well defended."

"And are we not?" Ann laughed.

"Oh, monstrous well defended, Cousin Ann."

Ann turned. Solomon and William were passing by, both bearing muskets, with Deb trailing behind with an armful of powder tubes.

Solomon swept off his hat to Ann.

"Oh, victory is certain now," he said to William. "Now the ladies are here to help us . . . nay, Will, to lead us in the battle like Joan of Arc. Why, when Prince Maurice sees Captain Ann here, and Colonel Miss Deb, he will swoon, swoo-oo-oon with terror . . ."

He staggered about, pretending to faint. Even Master Sampson laughed a little.

But William didn't laugh. William had been very quiet for days now.

Ann shrugged. She couldn't worry about it. She had given up worrying about things. She'd tried so hard to keep out of the fighting, but it hadn't worked.

They'd held that council of war, and then they'd just dragged her in, made her do it. It was too difficult to stand out as different from everyone else any longer. Not with her mother telling her they must all do whatever her uncle asked, and Aunt Berridge talking about a headstrong wench who needed a good whipping, and Deb calling her a traitor to the rest of them . . . Perhaps if she'd been at home, it would have been different. But here where she was a guest, an outsider, in the midst of a desperate struggle, it was too hard. She'd given in. And now –

She had to admit it. She was almost enjoying it.

She turned back to Master Sampson.

"I think it is time to show myself to the enemy once more," she said.

That day Captain Pyne died of his wounds.

The Admiral had sent his private surgeon to see him and Aunt Berridge had nursed him day and night, but nothing could be done.

"He will be buried early tomorrow," said Uncle Thomas at supper. "Very, very early. Before the enemy is awake."

CHAPTER 8

No Respect

William sat on a flat gravestone in the churchyard, carving a dolphin from a piece of wood.

He was doing it by touch alone, because it was half-past three in the morning and black as pitch. Sol would have told him not to be silly, using a knife like that in the dark, but Sol wasn't here. He was inside the church with the others, at Captain Pyne's funeral.

William could hear their voices and see the torchlight through the windows. Captain Pyne would be safely buried before the fighting started up again.

William had had enough of fighting. He didn't even like the sound of gunfire now. It reminded him of that oarsman with his brains spilling out.

He ran his thumb along the dolphin's back to its tail. Nearly finished. Sol had told him about dolphins swimming for miles alongside ships crossing the ocean. Perhaps William would go to sea himself one day. Anyway, it would be good to have a carved dolphin of his own, to keep by his bed when he went home.

If he went home.

He put the knife down and sat hunched, hands round knees. If he was at home now, he'd be fast asleep, not sitting in a dark churchyard with only another day's fighting ahead of him. I ought to be at home, he thought. I ought to go back to school.

He thought of his schoolmates safe back in Somerset, and wondered if he'd ever see them again.

A woman with a lantern was coming into the churchyard. Her man's black hat was slightly crooked. He watched her with irritation.

Women fighting, he thought. Dressing up like men as if they were playing a game. Fighting wasn't a game. He knew that now. Nothing had gone right since women had come onto the Line.

Or was it since he'd seen that boat sunk?

"William?" A hand touched his shoulder. "Are you waiting for Sol? I've brought you some food."

It was Judah. She set down the lantern and unwrapped some bread.

The burial must be over. They were coming out of the church, carrying torches. Now the soldiers would fire a volley of shots round the town as a mark of respect to Captain Pyne. Then everyone could snatch a little sleep until the fighting began again.

Judah glanced at him. "Are you not hungry?"

He shrugged, watching the flames of the torches bobbing. "No."

"This siege will end," Judah said in her gentle voice. "Soon. When – "

"When what?" William picked up his knife and began carving again, carelessly this time. "When you women have fought off the enemy for us?"

"No." She turned a surprised face to him in the lantern light. "It will end when all of us together – "

But she never finished her sentence. The funeral volley rang out.

Crack. Crack. Crack.

Pause.

Crack. Crack. Crack.

Pause.

Crack. Crack . . .

BOOOOM. Enemy gunfire opened up. BOOM. BOOM. BOOM.

61

William's knife slipped. He jumped up, clutching his cut hand.

"They can't fire on us now," he cried. "We're having a funeral. Have they no respect? I told Sol they were a stinking rabble."

Dark figures were running in the churchyard. "To the Line!" they shouted. "All back to the Line."

There'd be no sleep now. Just more fighting. More death.

He ran with everyone else down the dark street. He saw Solomon ahead, flame streaming from his high-held torch. Behind him he could hear Judah's soft footfalls, running too. But he didn't slow down for her. Who needed women at a time like this?

The enemy were firing from east and west at the same time, the town trapped between, taking a terrible battering. By the time William and Judah arrived, panting, at the Line, Royalist troops had begun to break through the earthworks.

"Here, Will!" shouted Solomon, thrusting his torch into soft earth. "Here with me." There was no time for the long process of loading the muskets. The enemy were already starting to scale the walls with ladders.

"Rocks! Drop rocks on them," yelled Solomon. He scrabbled at the wall, dug out one of the rocks that strengthened it, balanced on the step and hurled it as hard as he could. They heard a scream.

"Got one." He grunted in satisfaction. "More,

quickly, Will, Judah."

William bent to gather more. The cut on his hand was throbbing. The sickness in his stomach had come back and his mind felt dizzy and empty. It was the middle of the night. He should be in bed.

Solomon hung over the wall. "Here comes another of the rats. More rocks, quick." His face in the torchlight looked almost rat-like itself. "Come *on*, Will!"

William's fingers wouldn't grip. Judah was pushing and rolling stones into a pile at her brother's feet.

"More . . ." Solomon jumped down. "Aye, Judah, that big one. Up now. . . Lift it . . ."

William watched the two of them tottering under the weight of a huge stone, heaving it up, balancing it on top of the wall. They rocked it once, twice. A stone like that would crush a man to pulp.

"Now – one . . . two . . ."

Not wanting to, feeling sicker than ever, William climbed up on the step with them and looked over the edge.

Just below him a man was clinging to a ladder, straining to climb higher, the long fair hair under the Royalist helmet falling over his face. He shook it back impatiently. He was so close to William that they could look into each other's eyes.

They looked at each other for what seemed like a long time. Then Rufus said, "William?"

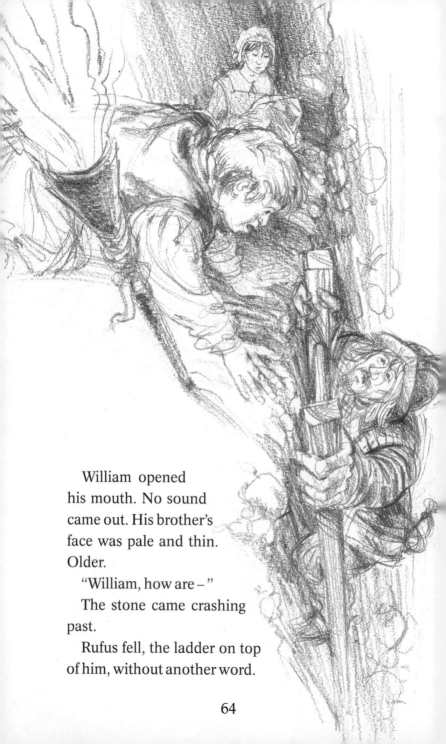

William opened
his mouth. No sound
came out. His brother's
face was pale and thin.
Older.

"William, how are –"

The stone came crashing
past.

Rufus fell, the ladder on top
of him, without another word.

After that everything in William's mind was mixed up. He knew he was shouting at Solomon about the fighting. About the stupid, stupid fighting that set people against each other and made them hurt each other and kill each other. About the King, and Parliament, and how he didn't care who won as long as it all stopped. About crushing men to death with stones, and about brains spilling out.

He was shouting at Judah too, about women fighting on the Line, dressing up like men, when they should be in the kitchen, not making everything worse.

He went on shouting and screaming and pummelling at the two of them while they tried to hold him still. Then he tore himself away, still shouting.

He ran and ran, sobbing and gasping, through the streets and alleys of the town until he ran straight into the imprisoning walls on the far side. Then he had to stop. There was nowhere else to go.

CHAPTER 9

Missing

William was missing. How *could* he be? wondered Ann as she hurried down the street. Lyme was under siege. Nobody could go out. So William must still be inside the walls.

But nobody had seen him since the early morning, when the Royalists had mistaken Lyme's funeral volley for an attack on them and a battle had started. And now it was evening.

Judah had told Ann about it.

Around midday she and Ann had been called away from the Line to the hospital. The fighting had been fierce and there were many casualties.

When they were side by side for a few moments, washing out a pile of bloodstained bandages, Judah had said, "Did you know that William . . . left the Line this morning, Ann? If you see him, tell him – "

"Left the Line?" Ann stared at her. "You mean he was wounded?"

"No," said Judah carefully. "He was upset. Shouting. Then he left."

"Without orders?" Ann couldn't believe it. "He ran away?"

"He left," Judah repeated. "But if you see him, Ann, tell him it's all right to come back. I'm sure it will be all right."

There was no more time to talk. Another cartload of wounded had arrived.

Ann couldn't stop thinking about it all day. Why would William be upset? How could he leave the Line and flee, run away like some conscripted enemy soldier? Nobody on their side did that, and especially not William. William loved it on the Line.

Or had done. She remembered his dispirited face lately, the way he hardly spoke to anyone.

Going back to Sherborne Lane for a quick supper, she kept looking for him – at his usual place on the Line, at Cobb Gate, in the streets. She asked people if they'd seen him. Nobody had.

He wasn't at supper either. But then, this was war-time. There was no more gathering round the meal table now while Uncle Thomas said grace. Everyone just ran into the house, snatched food where and when they could, and out again. William would appear soon.

He had to. For now she had something else to tell him, a piece of news he had to know. She must find him.

She was hurrying past the end of an alley when she saw him, huddled on a doorstep, head down.

"William?"

He looked up. "Go away."

Instead, she went nearer. He looked dreadful. His eyes were dull and lifeless.

"William, what happened on the Line this morning?"

He shrugged, staring down at his hand, wrapped round with a grubby kerchief.

"Aren't you going back? Judah said to tell you –"

"Oh, Judah," he muttered. "You women. We were all right as we were. You should have left the fighting to us. Everything's gone wrong since you women came into it."

"That's silly, William. You're just looking for someone to blame because you've got bored with it. You know the women are needed."

"You aren't. We'd have protected you, Sol and me. That's what men are for, to protect women. But you pushed in, dressed up in foolish hats. And before we knew it, huge great stones were – "

She shook her head. "You're mazed. You make no sense. But, William, there's something I must tell you." She looked straight at him. "In the hospital this afternoon, they brought in – "

"Rufus?" For a moment there was a spark of life in his eyes. "They brought in Rufus? Alive?"

She frowned.

"No, of course it wasn't Rufus. It was – "

"Sometimes they take in enemy soldiers when

68

they find them hurt. Perhaps when that stone fell, they took Rufus – "

"William," she said. "It wasn't Rufus."

"Then Rufus is dead." He turned away. "And Judah killed him."

"I know nothing about Rufus," said Ann. "It was Solomon they brought to the hospital this afternoon."

He stared at her.

"Solomon?"

She nodded. "Uncle and Aunt are with him now. He's very sick, William."

"Sick?" He looked dazed. "Why?"

"The earthworks collapsed. They'd pulled out too many stones. Solomon's leg was crushed."

"Sol's strong," said William. "He'll soon be back on the Line."

She shook her head. "William, they've had to – to cut the leg off to save his life. Solomon will never fight again. Or go to sea. He may not live."

She looked at him.

"He keeps asking for you," she said. "Come to the hospital now."

"Sol?"

Solomon was lying on a straw mattress, eyes open, staring at the ceiling. His big seafaring hands, fighting hands, were lying slack on the grey blanket. The blanket itself was raised by a cradle into a hump, keeping the weight from his lower body.

William tiptoed into the little circle of candle-light.

"Are you all right, Sol?"

Uncle Thomas, kneeling at his son's side, looked up and smiled bleakly.

"The Lord has carried him thus far, William," he said. "We must give thanks for that."

Kneeling on the other side, Aunt Berridge wiped Solomon's face.

"A moment only," she said. "He has drunk a

potion and he will sleep soon." She climbed stiffly to her feet. "Come, husband."

William waited for them to go. In the far corner Ann and Judah were easing a blood-soaked shirt away from a man's body, ignoring his groans and curses.

He turned back to Solomon. Even in candle-light his face looked grey.

"Sol . . ." He swallowed. "I'm sorry about your leg."

Solomon brought his gaze slowly down from the ceiling. He looked at William for a long moment with blurred, bloodshot eyes. Then he smiled.

"Aye, Cousin Will," he whispered. "'Tis gone. But I feel it still, kicking and jumping. Perhaps soon it will understand and . . . go away."

His eyes drooped. Then they opened again.

"This morning . . . " he said. "You ran away. Deserted your post."

The morning seemed far away now. The hot rage William had felt then had cooled like ashes.

"I'm sorry," he said. "But it was Rufus on that ladder."

"So you told us," Solomon said drily. "Perhaps if I had known . . . " He shifted a little and grimaced with pain. "But kill or be killed, that's war."

"Not if it's my brother," William protested.

"This is no foreign war," said Solomon. "In civil war, Will, we all fight one another. Besides, most soldiers are someone's brother. If you thought about that, perhaps you'd never fight at all."

"Perhaps." Sol could be saying something very important. He would think about it later. He was too tired now.

After a while Solomon said, "Now we are into this, we must win. Then it will stop. And Lyme can win. The women are like tigers." There was a ghost of his old grin.

"I hate women fighting," said William.

"So," said Solomon. "They will still fight. Some will even enjoy it. They'll find that battle can be sweet as well as sharp. But, Will – " He half sat up, grasping William's arm.

"Take my place on the Line. Help bring us peace. Lyme needs peace now, for us to lick our wounds, to count the cost and . . . and . . ." His eyes were closing again.

"Sol, look." William pulled out the wooden dolphin and pressed it into his cousin's hand. "For you. Take it when you go back to sea. You will go back, Sol, won't you?"

Solomon's fingers tightened on the carving, took hold.

"Aye," he whispered. "It is clean at sea. We are all brothers there, Will. All brothers."

His eyes closed and he slept.

CHAPTER 10

The World in Flames

Far away, His Majesty King Charles sat at his writing desk, drumming his thin fingers.

"What ails my nephew? He has been encamped now on the Dorset cliffs for over five weeks. He has troops a-plenty, the finest artillery. Yet still Lyme laughs in his face!

"You recall that we wrote in February to Sir John Stawell requiring him to send two hundred foot soldiers to help bring that rebellious town of Lyme into subjection. And many other gentlemen have sent their armies too. What more does my nephew need?"

His secretary gave a little cough. "I understand, your Majesty, that Prince Maurice has been suffering from the new disease, the influenza. No doubt that has made the task difficult."

The King stared at him, cold-eyed. "The task was simple," he said. "We are most disappointed in him."

Was it this news of the King's disappointment, coming as May was turning into June, that made Prince Maurice try one last desperate idea?

Charles R.

Trusty & welbeloved Wee greete you well. Whereas Wee vnderstand yᵉ Condicōn of yᵉ rebellious Towne of Lyme to be such, as (by Gods blessing) yᵉ present addicōn of some fewe more foote Forces may bring the same into Our Subiecōn & Obedience: Wee haue therefore thought fitt to require you forthwith to send twoe hundred of yoᵉ foote togethᵉr with their Armes & Pay to that Work (the like whereof Wee haue ordered Cᵒᵗᵉᵈᵉ . Wyndham to doe also) to be returned back again to you at the end of that Service, weᶜʰ Wee conceaue & hope wilbe speedily. And hereof Wee desire you by noe meanes to faile: And these Our Letters shalbe yᵉ Warrant on that behalfe. Given at Our Court at Oxford yᵉ 11ᵗʰ day of february 1643.

By his Maᵗⁱᵉˢ Comand

Edw: Nicholas

*The original letter sent by King Charles I
to Sir John Stawell*

Ann and Deb were on the river-bank when it started.

"To the river with you," Aunt Berridge had ordered that morning, pushing a bundle of stockings and shirts and petticoats into Ann's arms as they left the house.

"But we are needed on the Line, Mother," Deb had pouted.

"Fiddlesticks. The guns are quiet today. And clothes must still be washed, siege or no siege. To the river, and womanly work for once."

Deb had grumbled all morning.

"They will miss us on the Line." She sat on the river-bank, splashing her feet, watching the kneeling Ann haul a wet shirt out on to a flat stone and start to pound it. "Does Mother ask William to do such silly work? No, never. He goes to the Line every morning now, and yet we girls are taken away from fighting. Is it not unfair, Ann? When fighting is so . . ."

"So exciting," said Ann.

She felt guilty saying it. But it was the most exciting thing she'd ever done.

"Yes, exciting," said Deb. "Washing clothes in war-time is foolish. They'll be dirty again in a moment."

She hooked her hand behind her and dragged the rest of the clothes into the shallow river. "Let them lie there and soak. You and I, Ann, will take a swim."

"Oh, Deb, no . . ."

But Deb was already throwing off her shoes and stockings, tucking up her skirts and wading away down river, laughing over her shoulder.

"Can't catch me! Catch me, Ann."

"I'm coming. Wait . . ."

The two girls ran kicking and splashing through the sunlit water, all thoughts of the siege forgotten. Soon their skirts were drenched and they were helpless with laughter.

"Oh, Deb." Ann collapsed on the grass. "If your mother could see us."

"Or the preachers. All those preachers who have packed into Lyme, telling us we are doing the Lord's work." Deb placed her palms together and rolled her eyes skywards. "Do you know, Ann, people say there are at least five-and-twenty of them here at the moment – "

She broke off.

"Ann, what is that? Look." She pointed to the west of the town. "That's not gun smoke."

Red and yellow flames were shooting up into the sky. Ann scrambled to her feet.

"It's a roof on fire. And, see, another over there."

"Ann! Deb!"

They turned round. Their two mothers were panting along the lane towards them with empty, clanking buckets.

"Water!" Aunt Berridge called. "All the water you can carry, fast, fast."

"What's happened?"

"They're firing flaming arrows." Mistress Say was scooping up water. "Setting roofs ablaze. In this dry weather it will spread . . ."

Already they could see several cottages blazing in the distance.

"Quickly, girls, quickly . . . Fill the buckets . . . Oh, the Lord have mercy . . . !"

For the rest of that dreadful Saturday they fetched water from the river, from the sea, from wells. And still the arrows kept falling.

No sooner had they dowsed the flames from one thatched roof than another silent, deadly arrow would fall from the sky and set another blazing. Fire leapt from roof to roof across the narrow streets. Red-hot fragments whirled in the air.

"Water, more water . . ."

"Where's the water cart?"

"Pass buckets. Form a chain there . . ."

"Keep it from the powder store. Dear God, not the powder store . . ."

Ann coughed and choked on the black smoke, her eyes streaming, her face scorched. How can they do this to us? she thought. Do they not know there are people down here?

"Ann." Her mother tore off her kerchief, thrust it into a bucket of water and tossed it to her. "Cover your mouth with that. Then help me with this ladder." She was dragging a heavy ladder towards a blazing roof.

"What are you doing? Don't, Mother. Don't go up there."

"I must. I must pull the thatch down. I know how to do it. Give me that rake, quickly, girl."

Ann strained her eyes upwards as her mother climbed. A flash of memory came to her: she was a tiny girl, at home on the farm, watching through the window. Her mother was holding a ladder while her father climbed to put out a fire in a hayrick, pulling the thatch down with a rake . . .

"Stand back below!"

Bundles of blazing thatch tumbled to the ground.

Women stamped out the flames, threw water, choking on the hissing, reeking smoke.

"Stand back below!"

Against the sky the roof spars reared scorched and blackened as more thatch was pulled down.

Crack. Crack. Crack. Three shots rang out. There was a scream from the top of the ladder.

"Mother!"

Aunt Berridge pushed Ann aside. "They're firing on us, may they be forgiven. I must reach your mother . . ."

From the Line, it seemed to William that the whole world was going up in flames. Throughout the day the defenders stood at their posts as the houses burned around them. They choked in smoke, hearing the shots and the women's screams.

"Stand firm." The order was passed down the Line. "The enemy may try to break through at any moment. Stand firm whatever befalls."

William stood firm. He hated the fighting now, but there was to be no more shouting, no more running away. He stood at Sol's place in the Line, gripping Sol's musket, ready to fire when the order came, calm and ready. He did it for Sol and, in a strange way, for Rufus.

"Good lad," said Master John Sampson. "Good lad."

Many women were injured. It was midnight before the fires were damped down and Mistress Say's burns could be dressed.

"Ah." Aunt Berridge unwrapped the blackened rags. "You will bear the scars a long time, I fear."

"I ducked to avoid the shots," said Mistress Say, wincing with pain, "and clutched the burning thatch to save myself. So foolish."

"Not foolish." Aunt Berridge bent over her collection of herbs. "You were the bravest of us all."

Ann looked at her aunt. To her surprise she saw tears in her eyes.

The fire attacks went on and grew worse, and still Lyme stood. And deserters began to trickle away from Prince Maurice.

On 5th June two Royalists, a sergeant and a corporal, deserted from the King's army and came into town. The Governor questioned them. They told him that, since Prince Maurice could not conquer Lyme, he had decided to destroy it.

"See, 'tis like a last ditch stand," explained the corporal. "They know they've lost in all but name, so they reckon to go out on a blaze of glory, like." They would set the whole town ablaze, he said.

"Indeed?" said the Governor. "Even the stone-roofed houses?"

"Ah," said the sergeant. "But they've got a witch up there in one of the camps. They say she can do anything. Set stone ablaze, sink all those ships out in the bay . . ."

A quiver of fear went round the listeners.

"Superstitious nonsense," said the Governor firmly. "Take them away."

It wasn't only fire-arrows now. As the hot June days dragged by it was sometimes red-hot bullets or hooked iron bars that caught in the thatch and could not be dislodged. Smoke hung in the air day and night.

But Lyme was battle-hardened now. Nothing could break its spirit. There would be no deserters from the Lyme ranks.

It would stand firm till the very end.

CHAPTER 11

Wait for the Morrow

And the end was coming.

It was hard to tell it inside the walls. The fire attacks came day after weary day, and the guns were never quiet. They were beginning to run short of gunpowder again. Inside the walls were injury, disease and death. Death, like the heavy smoke clouds, hung over the little town.

And yet, there were signs the end was coming.

It was Friday 14th June. Ann was on duty at one of the forts.

"Here, maid, take over." A soldier thrust his musket at her and stood up, stretching. "Just a moment or two."

There were few jokes now about women fighting.

Ann took up position at the firing slit, the heavy musket as familiar in her hands as a broom. How they'd all changed, she thought, catching sight of her black, greasy hands on the gun.

She sat scanning the enemy fields. There were people in the distance who seemed to be arguing, picking things up and putting them down again.

She watched them coming nearer. It could be the start of a new attack.

"All well, maid?" asked the soldier, coming back.

"Look at these people," said Ann. "The front one's carrying something."

The soldier squinted through the slit.

"It's a white flag," he said. "Maybe they wants a parley. But there's a lot of them, at least a score, I reckon. And, see, two of them's women. What are they about?"

William, coming into the fort with a fresh supply of powder, ran right into them at the gate.

"Captain Phere of His Majesty's army," the leader

was introducing himself to the fort commander. He laid down his makeshift white flag and his sword, and turned to the two women behind him. "My wife," he said. "Her maid-servant."

The women's gowns were tattered and stained, but they held their heads high, staring round proudly.

The fort commander bowed slightly. "You wish to surrender?" he asked.

"It is all but over," Captain Phere said. His face was weary. "We had such high hopes. But we have lost so many. Too many. It must stop."

"What's happening?" William whispered to a corporal.

"They're deserters," muttered the corporal with disgust. "Rats leaving the sinking ship."

The commander swung round. "Silence, you two. Go and disarm those men coming through."

William looked at the straggle of men behind Captain Phere. They seemed little different from their own soldiers.

"Right, over here," ordered the corporal. "In a line."

Tiredly the men filed past, dropping their muskets and pikes at William's feet, emptying out their pockets for the corporal. Many had bandaged heads or arms, several hobbled on crutches.

The corporal followed them into the fort and saluted.

"Twenty-five enemy deserters, sir. All searched and correct."

William lingered outside, looking across the barricades to enemy ground. There was someone else out there, very close, sitting at the base of an oak tree, staring across at the fort. Wondering whether to desert or not, William guessed. Then the man flicked back his hair and saw William watching him.

A smile slowly spread across his face. He raised his arm and beckoned.

"Ann! Where's Ann?"

William raced through the fort and tugged at Ann's hand.

"Rufus is alive, Ann!" He couldn't take it in. "He's not dead, he's out there, waiting to come over. Come and talk to him, Ann. He wants to surrender."

"We can't cross the Line." Ann looked dazed. "We'll be shot."

"We must. He's our brother. He wants to talk to us."

"But – "

The soldier at the firing slit lowered his musket.

"Go over, maid," he said. "Civil war is a pesky business sometimes. Brother on one side, sister on t'other. Go over. We'll not shoot, will we, lads?"

They sat close together under the oak tree, Rufus and Ann and William, talking of home.

"The farm is ruined," said William. "They cut down the trees, slaughtered the animals . . ."

"Who?"

"Soldiers."

"King's soldiers?"

"No. Parliament."

"No difference," Rufus said. Then he said, "And Mother? How does she do?"

They told him how she'd climbed to put out the thatch fires.

"Her hands were burnt," said Ann. "Burnt almost away . . ." She stopped, seeing Rufus's face change, tighten up with pain.

"I would like to see her," said Rufus.

Silence fell between them.

"Rufus," said William at last. "When you were trying to cross the trench that day, and the stone fell – "

"It hit the ladder, not me," said Rufus. "But I fell too. With good fortune, on something soft."

"What?"

"One of our troopers." Rufus smiled briefly. "He had just made the same descent."

"Oh," said William. "Was he all right?"

"No, he was dead."

Another silence. Smoke drifted across the hazy sea. A kestrel was circling above a clump of bramble bushes. Rufus watched it through narrowed eyes.

"One day we'll plant trees at home," he said. "And buy more animals. When all this is over."

"They say the siege will end soon," said William.

"Aye." Rufus's mouth twisted wryly. "We make much noise to keep up our spirits, but we are hard pressed. We have too many men we have forced to fight whose hearts are not with us. But the war will go on. On and on, until there are no more towns to conquer and no more people to kill, and His Majesty is safe upon his throne once more."

"Or until he has learnt a lesson," William was

88

about to say. Then he changed his mind and said nothing.

"Rufus," said Ann. "Come over to our side. They've promised you'll be well treated. Come over with us now."

Rufus smiled at her. "A hand, I beg you, sister."

She helped him up. He grunted with pain.

"Cracked ribs," he explained. "That trooper was a more bony man than I thought."

He glanced back at the Royalist camp. They were taking down tents. "It is time to go," he said. "Give Mother my love and – my regrets."

"Come with us," begged William.

"And be a deserter?" asked Rufus. "A turncoat? Betray my king because a battle is lost? He will need all the friends he can muster."

He put one arm round Ann's shoulders, the other round William's, and gave them a hard hug.

"We'll plant those trees, you and Mother and I," he said. "We will sit on our own land and watch them grow. Just wait for the morrow."

They nodded.

He limped away, back to his own camp, and they stood watching him until he was out of sight.

CHAPTER 12

The Sun in the Morning

Few people in Lyme slept that night. The town was buzzing with talk.

Some people said the attacks were as bad as ever. A red-hot iron bar had fallen through a roof onto a bed where five children were sleeping. It was simply by the mercy of God that only one child had been slightly hurt.

Yes, said others. But what of the columns of marching soldiers, the carriages full of King's officers and their wives, that had been spotted hurrying off along the Uplyme road towards Exeter? What of those huge guns on the cliffs? Surely they were being dismantled, dragged away? Surely that wasn't imagination?

The siege was coming to an end.

Wasn't it?

"Look," said William.

It was the middle of the night. The whole Berridge household had been too restless to sleep, and he and Ann had slipped out for a while. They leaned over the sea wall at Cobb Gate.

"Look down there." William pointed.

A little boat was being rowed ashore through a silver-white path of moonlight.

"They're bringing stores off from one of the ships," said Ann.

"I know," said William. "But listen."

She listened. It was so quiet she could hear the dip and lift of the oars.

"Listen to what?" she asked.

"To the quiet," he said. "The enemy haven't fired on that boat. There's no firing. I think they've given up."

"And day will soon be coming," said Ann.

They walked back to the Line, not talking. The terrible pictures that William had carried in his mind slipped away at last. It was Saturday 15th June, just eight weeks since Prince Maurice had arrived on the cliffs above Lyme and begun the siege.

"Give them a burst of fire," said Uncle Thomas a few hours later. "Let us hear their reply."

"Aye, Master Berridge."

William glanced up at the cliffs, silent and empty against the early morning sky. Then he looked along the Line, where people stood motionless, tense.

"What think you, Will?" murmured a voice behind him. "Has the gallant prince left us at last?"

"Sol!"

He turned round to see Solomon, with Judah on one side of him, Deb on the other. He was propped up on crutches, the stump of his leg was heavily bandaged, his face pale. But he was smiling.

"I thought you would stay a-bed," said William.

"A-bed? On such a great day?" He shook his head. "Not I. Now hush."

"FIRE!"

A volley of shots rang out in a burst of smoke. Then silence.

"They've gone – " Ann began.

Solomon put out an arm to hold her back.

"AGAIN!"

Another volley. More smoke. And, again, silence. Then . . .

"Very well," said Uncle Thomas. "I think we can say – "

His voice was lost in wave after wave of cheering. All along the Line people dropped their weapons, hugged each other, wept with relief.

"Thank God, thank God." Mistress Say covered her face with her bandaged hands.

"Come, cousins," said Solomon.

Shuffling, hopping, scrambling, he led the four of them across the earthworks into a trampled green field, wet with dew. The enemy trenches lay silent and deserted. A thin dog rooted among the scattered debris. A rusting helmet lay upturned; someone had dropped a half-chewed apple in the mud.

"They've gone!"

"Gone!"

Laughing and breathless, they began to stumble uphill. Higher and higher they climbed, up one steep field, across another, all of them helping Solomon along.

Ann drew a deep breath of clean fresh air, free at last from the stench of gunpowder and burning thatch. She turned round, walking backwards, and saw the smoke rolling away from the town below, and a blue patch of sky clearing above the sea. Over their heads, a blackbird began to sing.

"O give thanks unto the Lord . . ."

As they came to the top of the cliffs they saw a preacher had gathered a little crowd around him, and was reading to them from his pocket Bible:

"O give thanks to him that gave great lights . . .
The sun to rule by day:
The moon and stars to rule by night . . ."

Should I have fought? Ann thought. I was so sure at the beginning. War was stupid, war was wrong. And then I joined in. If I'd said no, if we'd all said no, there would have been no fighting and perhaps people wouldn't have died. But what would have happened to Lyme?

She looked down at the battered little town, the criss-cross of trenches and the ruined houses.

I'll never forget these weeks, she told herself. Never.

The preacher's voice rose:

"To him that smote great kings . . .
And hath redeemed us from our enemies:
Who remembered us in our low estate;
O give thanks to the God of heaven
For his mercy endureth for ever."

"Now we will go home," said William. "Soon, soon. I have had enough of fighting. Even though the war goes on, we will go home."

"And I to sea," said Solomon. He took the wooden dolphin from his pocket. "You must carve me a good seafaring leg, Will, one that will grip the deck on stormy nights."

A sweep of gulls rose from the sea, circled the cliffs and wheeled out across the bay.

Trudging the long road out of Lyme with the rest of the defeated King's forces, Rufus saw them fly, and saw how their wings were touched with silver in the clear morning light. His heart lifted.

One day they would plant those trees, and sit together on their own land and watch them grow.

One day.